GROWIN'

"Hey kid." I turned around. It was the boy who sat next to me in class.

"You're new, aren't you, Yo-lan-da?" He stretched my name out so that I could tell he was making fun of me.

"Don't call me Yolanda," I said boldly. "My name is Pump. And don't you forget it." I was trying real hard to sound tough so that he would leave me alone. But he didn't believe me.

"I'll call you Yo-lan-da as much as I feel like it. What are you goin' to do about it?" he said, and he was looking mean. Well, I knew I wasn't going to get out of a fight, so I put my books down on the ground and tried not to shake so much from being scared.

Growin'

Nikki Grimes

PUFFIN BOOKS

PUFFIN BOOKS

Published by the Penguin Group

Penguin Books USA Inc., 375 Hudson Street, New York, New York 10014, U.S.A.

Penguin Books Ltd, 27 Wrights Lane, London W8 5TZ, England

Penguin Books Australia Ltd, Ringwood, Victoria, Australia

Penguin Books Canada Ltd, 10 Alcorn Avenue, Toronto, Ontario, Canada M4V 3B2

Penguin Books (N.Z.) Ltd, 182-190 Wairau Road, Auckland 10, New Zealand

Penguin Books Ltd, Registered Offices: Harmondsworth, Middlesex, England

First published in the United States of America by the Dial Press, 1977

Published in Puffin Books, 1995

1 3 5 7 9 10 8 6 4 2

THE LIBRARY OF CONGRESS HAS CATALOGED THE DIAL PRESS EDITION AS FOLLOWS:

Grimes, Nikki.

Growin'.

Summary: Pump thinks her world has ended when her father,

the only person who believed in her poetry,

suddenly dies. That is, until she meets Jim Jim.

[1. Friendship—Fiction.] I. Lilly, Charles. II. Title. PZ7.G88429Gr [Fic]

77-71518 ISBN 0-8037-3272-4 ISBN 0-8037-3273-2 lib. bdg.

Puffin Books ISBN 0-14-037066-8

Printed in the United States of America

For Jesus Christ who brought me through
And for Tawfiqa who was sent to light the way

Growin'

I'm Black. You don't like that, do you?
Liar. Who's that I see layin' on the beach
with suntan lotion? Is that you?

"Pump! Didn't you hear me call you to dinner? What are you doin'?" Mama's footsteps were almost at my door. I dug into my army bag and felt around for the history book. I flipped it open and shoved my poetry notebook between the pages. Mama pushed open the door.

"I asked you what you were doin', girl. I called you three times already!"

I held the book straight up so she could see the cover. I prayed ahead of time so Jesus wouldn't be mad at me.

"I'm studyin'." It wasn't a big lie. I was, sort of. I was studying how to finish that poem. Mama didn't believe me. Before I knew anything, she had walked over to my bed and snatched that book right out of my hands. When she saw the poem her face screwed up like a raisin.

"Humph. I see you're still wastin' time writin' this mumbo jumbo." I wanted to cuss Mama for that. I had to bite my lip to keep from saying something nasty. She hurt me and I wanted to hurt her right back. Just wait, I thought. Just wait till I tell Daddy.

"Put those books away, go wash your hands, and come to the table," Mama said, throwing my book on top of my army bag like my poem was a sour-smelling leftover. I piled the books up on my dresser and went to the bathroom. I ran the water full blast so that you couldn't hear anything else from outside. I couldn't hold it back no more, so I cried. I cried because she didn't love me. My own

Mama. I loved my poetry and she hated what I loved. It came to the same thing. So I cried. When I finished, I washed my face so Mama couldn't see where I'd been crying. I didn't want her to know that I even cared. I dried my hands and face and went to dinner.

The next afternoon I sat in my room, all mopey, rolling a marble back and forth. Daddy worked nights, so he was still home. He came in and sat down beside me on the floor without saying anything. Then he put his hand underneath my chin and made me look in his eyes.

"What's the matter, Pumpkin?" His voice was soft. I got up, went to the dresser, and brought back my history book. I shook out my notebook of poetry and handed it to him in silence. He read it and smiled to himself.

"It's only half finished," I said.

"Why don't you finish it?" he asked. I shrugged my shoulders, trying to look cool.

"Mama said it was just some ol' mumbo jumbo, so I . . ."

"Oh, so *that's* it," he said, losing his smile. "Well, I don't think she really meant that, Pumpkin." I loved my Daddy and I didn't want to call him a liar. But I didn't believe any of that stuff about Mama not meaning what she said.

"Can I have your poem?" he asked. I shrugged my shoulders again.

"Sure."

He tore the page from the notebook, folded it carefully, and slipped it into his shirt pocket.

"Now, how about some handball?" he asked, with his eyes all shiny. My mouth stopped frowning when my ears heard that. He knew I loved to play handball.

"Right now?" I asked.

"Right now." He smiled back.

I ducked under my bed and hunted for my sneakers.

Spring was just starting, so it was still a little cool. We had on Windbreakers that weren't really that warm, but once we got to playing we were hot enough to take them off. We played and talked at the same time.

"Pumpkin," Daddy started. "You have to try and understand your mama. She's not like us exactly. She likes music and poetry all right."

I looked at him as if to say, Oh yeah?

"It's just that your mother worries about money.

She thinks that goin' to school and gettin' a job is the most important thing. You have to make a livin' no matter what. She doesn't have anything against you personally."

"Mama can't stand me, and you know it!" I burst out. "Nothin' I do ever pleases her. Not even good grades in school. Instead of seein' how well I did in English, she harps on how bad I did in math. I passed, didn't I? But that's not good enough. It's never good enough. She . . ."

I had run out of breath, talking all at once like that. I had forgotten about the game and let the ball go. I looked around for it. It had rolled close to the curb. I picked it up and threw it against the wall of the school building, starting the game up again.

"Your mother loves you, Pumpkin," said Daddy. "Just as much as I do. Maybe more. . . ." That was all he said.

We played for a half hour or so and went home. Daddy sent me upstairs and he got into our old rattletrap Volkswagen and headed for work.

I was dreaming that I was the only person in a roller coaster at Coney Island. I was all the way at the top and could see people on the ground like little dots. The car stayed at the top for a minute and I closed my eyes real tight to keep from looking down. The coaster started again, slowly rolling over the edge. That's when I heard Mama scream and woke up.

I ran to Mama's room to see what was wrong. When I got there, she was sitting on her bed, very still and quiet. Her eyes were faraway, like she had forgotten where she was. Her face was all wet from crying.

I just stood at the door, looking. I was too scared to go to her, and too scared to leave her all alone. I'd never seen her that way before.

When she noticed me standing there, she wiped her face so that I wouldn't know she was crying. It was too late, but I didn't say anything.

"Honey," said Mama. "Come here. Mama has to tell you somethin'."

You never call me Honey, I thought. And why can't you tell me whatever it is from over there? But I didn't ask any questions out loud. I just did what she said. When I got close, she put her arms around me and hugged me to her chest, like she was afraid I'd run away.

"Daddy won't be comin' home anymore," she began. "He had a bad car accident tonight and he . . . died."

Right then I knew why Mama was holding me so tight. I did want to run away. I wanted to run as far and as fast as I could and never stop to rest or think or anything. And if my daddy really wasn't coming home anymore, then I'd keep running and never come back. Never.

Mama and I had never talked much, and we still didn't. But some things changed between us. She kept trying to get close to me, and I kept moving farther away. In between all the rushing around to put the funeral together, and packing up everything after so we could move, Mama kept hugging me and holding my hand every chance she got, and saying that now all we had was each other. And every chance I got, I'd run and hide in some corner and cry and be mad at Daddy for leaving me, and mad at Mama for still being alive when she knew I loved Daddy best, and mad at God cause it was His doing.

When all the fuss died down two weeks later, I went to visit my best friend, Cherry. By that time Cherry and everybody else in the world knew what had happened, so I didn't have to tell her. It was just as well, because I wasn't much for talking.

Mama was all packed up before I knew anything, and it was time to move. Mama didn't want to live in the same place where Daddy had been, and I didn't want to live anywhere else. But my not agreeing didn't stop us from moving any. I remember how it was when I told Cherry.

"Movin' is dumb," Cherry grumbled. We'd been playing handball in the school yard and it was way past time for us to be going home. She stuffed the ball into her pocket and we started down the block.

"Damn," Cherry cussed, sucking her teeth. "You shouldn't go nowhere you can't take your friends." There wasn't anything to say, so I just smiled a little and squeezed her hand. We took the slow way home and kicked a rock back and forth between us all the way. We must've worn that rock out.

Now, here we were in a new apartment, in a new neighborhood. I hated Mama sometimes.

"Pumpkin," called Mama. "Time for school, girl. Get ready."

I knelt on a stack of unpacked boxes and stared out the window of my new "home." I frowned, angry because I didn't know any of the people who passed by and they didn't know me. I hated them for being strangers. I hated everyone that morning.

"Pumpkin!"

"Comin', comin'," I yelled. I strolled into the bathroom and ran the water lukewarm. I rubbed the soap to make bubbles. I looked through the water stopped up in the sink and studied the unfamiliar cracks and stains. Even the sink was strange. I stuck my finger in and twirled the water around and around. In the old house, I would wash up in such a hurry that I always forgot to clean my ears, and Mama would send me back to the bathroom to wash all over again. Cherry would be waiting for me on the stoop every morning.

We'd race each other to school and the last one there had to carry the other's books all day long. Sometimes after school, we'd buy an ice-cream sandwich or two-scoop cone and split it. We'd be licking that cone at the same time with our heads butting each other, and laughing while the ice cream melted and trickled over our fingers. . . . Cherry was the closest I came to having a sister. She was part of my morning. But not this morning. It was the first day in the new school and I didn't want to go. Cherry wouldn't be there. So I washed real slow the way Mama was always scolding me to.

Maybe, I thought, if I take a long time getting ready, it will be too late to go to school today. But just then Mama called for me to hurry up, and I knew for sure that I wasn't gonna get my wish.

Mama had to walk to school with me to register. School was only four blocks away but it felt like at least a trillion miles. Whenever we passed a group of people, everyone stopped talking and you could almost hear all the questions going through their minds, waiting to burst out of their mouths soon as you passed by. "Who are they? They come from around here? They move here by themselves? That child got a father?" And you could feel their pop eyes studying you from head to foot, without even looking. Soon as we walked farther on, the group started up talking again, and I didn't have to imagine about what. Mama pretended not to notice, and I made believe I didn't care. But I don't think either of us fooled anybody.

I was the first one in school when the bell rang. I went straight to the back of the room and took the seat nearest the window. When everyone was sitting, the teacher took attendance. She read through all the names, one right after another, until she got to mine.

"Yolanda Jackson," called the teacher.

"Here," I said, sucking my teeth. Nobody ever called me Yolanda. Not since I was a baby. They used to call me Pumpkin, then they made it Pump. But nobody knew that here.

The class was noisy. Mrs. Lee, the teacher, tapped her ruler on the desk. Then she did exactly what I hoped she wouldn't.

"Class," she said, "I want you all to say hello to Yolanda. She's new here, and I want you to make friends."

Oh, Lord, I thought. I wanted to scream, I don't care if you make friends or not. You don't like me, I don't like you. I hate everybody. My daddy's dead and you don't understand and I hate everybody. See? I should have screamed. I didn't.

All of the kids turned in their seats to look at me. Half of them rolled their eyes in my direction and turned away, bored. The others stared me up and down till I felt like a speck underneath a microscope. I wished I really was that small just then so that I could hide. But I couldn't, so I just slid down in my seat until all you could see over the desk was the top of my head. I waited for Mrs. Lee to scold me and make me sit up straight but, thank God, she just went on calling the roll.

The boy sitting next to me acted like the teacher had given him a license to watch me all day long, 'cause that's exactly what he did. He watched and doodled something on his desk. He never opened his mouth, never let me see what he was doodling, and he never cracked the tiniest smile. He made me nervous. Later on I found out I had a good reason to be. He was the class bully.

When I was standing on line in the cafeteria I heard some scuffling up in front.

"I said *move.*" It was the boy who sat next to me in class.

"But I was standin' here first! You can't get ahead of me."

"Listen, kid, why don't you get out of here before I punch you out."

A couple of kids whistled, and somebody said, "Ooh, wolf!" but nobody moved. The boy who'd been pushed out of line was little for his age but he was in our class. He looked scared and confused. Without saying anything he was begging for help.

"You better do what he says," came the only advice.

The bully crossed his arms, looking like the Hulk from the comic books, rolled his eyes, and squeezed his mouth shut so tight, no air could get inside. Before I knew anything, that little boy was shaking and crying all at the same time.

The "Hulk" let his arms fall to his side, took a long, tired breath, and stepped out of line.

"Here, kid," he said, like he was one of them welfare workers who act like the money they're giving away is their own. "You can have your ol' place. Just consider yourself lucky." He turned and walked toward the back of the line with his head bent down. When he got close to me he raised his head, and he had this holding-in look like he wanted to laugh or something. I looked after him for a while, but then the line started moving, and besides, I couldn't figure out what was funny.

The rest of the day was quiet for me. Nobody wanted to waste their time talking to a dumb new kid who didn't know their games or their secrets. Once, while the teacher was on English, I closed my eyes real tight and prayed hard to disappear in a puff of smoke and to all of a sudden be back in my old classroom with my friends. Then I waited and waited. Finally I opened my eyes to see if it had worked. If Cherry was there, then it worked. But there sat that same boy, the class bully.

"Movin' is dumb," I mumbled, and looked out the window until the bell rang.

When school let out, I headed straight home. I wasn't too keen on hanging around the school yard yet. One thing I knew from watching kids move to my old block was that every time you move to a new neighborhood, sooner or later somebody picks a fight with you to see if you'll stand up for yourself. I didn't like fights very much, especially if I was in one, and even though I knew that one day I'd have to get it over with, I sure wasn't in no hurry.

I walked fast with my head down low so I couldn't see anyone. I bumped into a pole twice, but it was better than having a run-in with some kid itching for a fight. When I got to the corner I stopped to wait for the light to turn green. I thought I heard someone come up behind me. But I didn't look back. I couldn't wait for the light to change. It was taking a million years. I took a deep breath and ran into the street.

"Hey! What's wrong with you kids?" someone yelled from a car. I turned to say I was sorry and was nearly hit by another car. Horns were honking all over the place, and everybody was yelling at me to get out of the street. When I got to the other side, I slowed down so I could catch my breath. I should have kept running. Someone tapped me on the shoulder.

"Hey, kid." I turned around. It was the boy who sat next to me in class.

"You're new, aren't you, Yo-lan-da?" He

stretched my name out so that I could tell he was making fun of me.

"Don't call me Yolanda," I said boldly. "My name is Pump. And don't you forget it." I was trying real hard to sound tough so that he would leave me alone. But he didn't believe me.

"I'll call you Yo-lan-da as much as I feel like it. What are you goin' to do about it?" he said, and he was looking mean. Well, I knew I wasn't going to get out of a fight, so I put my books down on the ground and tried not to shake so much from being scared.

Then I made myself look him in the eye.

"If you call me Yo-lan-da again, I'll push you, that's what." He still didn't believe me.

"I dare you," he said. Everybody knew you were scared if you backed down from a dare, and they would pick on you for the rest of your life. So I pushed him as hard as I could. I waited for him to push back, but he didn't.

"I dare you to do it again," he said. My knees weren't knocking exactly, they just rattled a little. But I pushed him again.

"I dare you to do it again," he said. So I pushed him a third time and waited for him to kill me.

Instead he bent down and picked up my books from the ground. Then he broke out in a big sunshine smile.

"My name is Jim Jim," he said. "Welcome to the block, Pump."

I saw Jim Jim a lot after that. We usually sat together at lunch and then we'd meet after school to play stickball. Sometimes we'd visit each other's house.

I liked visiting with Jim Jim at his house because there were always so many other kids around. Being an only child was all right, I guess, but whenever I saw Jim Jim laughing and teasing with his brothers and sisters I wished I came from a big family too.

Jim Jim's mother was on welfare, but she worked waiting tables three days a week off the record and Jim Jim would have to baby-sit when he came home from school. She had six kids including Jim Jim and needed all the money she could get.

Jim Jim used to fuss up a storm about how he couldn't stand baby-sitting all those snotty-nose brats. But I never paid him no mind 'cause soon as one of them looked like he was even thinking about crying, Jim Jim was there hugging him all up. He was the oldest and his Mama called him the man of the family cause Jim Jim's daddy had left them a long time before. Jim Jim said he left 'cause he never could get a good-enough job to feed all those kids. Jim Jim said that was no reason to his way of thinking. But that didn't matter, 'cause he was already gone, wasn't he? I think Jim Jim liked having his Mama call him the man of the house though.

One thing I never could understand was how Jim Jim could be so sweet to his brothers and sisters, even when they were a pain, and then turn right around and be mean to some kid at school who never did anything to him. One day when we were having lunch at school, I asked him about that.

That day we had chop suey for lunch. It wasn't really chop suey but that's what they called it. It looked like mush to me, but all the same, Jim Jim was digging into it.

I closed my eyes and tried to make believe I didn't know what the food looked like so I could eat it. But it didn't work, so I pushed my plate away and just looked around the lunchroom to see who was there. Coming in at the door, I saw the same little boy Jim Jim had pushed out of line my first day in school.

"Jim Jim," I said. "Why you play like you're so mean all the time?"

Jim Jim paid me no mind and went right on eating.

"Come on, Jim Jim. You know you ain't really mean, so why you act like that?"

Jim Jim looked up from his plate. "I am so mean," he said. Then he rolled his eyes and did his teeth like Dracula to prove it. I almost laughed myself underneath the table.

"Jim Jim, stop. I'm serious," I said, still laughing. "Really, you so sweet and soft with the kids at home and all. But in school, can't nobody even say hello to you without gettin' growled at except me. I don't understand that," I said, and waited for his answer.

Jim Jim finished his chop suey and looked up at me. He stared at me for a long time like he was making up his mind whether to tell me or to start in on my chop suey.

"If you really want to know . . . it goes back to

when I was in first grade. I used to be real quiet then. I would come to school and do my work and wouldn't talk to nobody, wouldn't bother nobody.

"Then this kid named Tyrone from second grade come pushin' on me in the school yard one day. I hadn't done anything to him. I didn't even know him and here he was tryin' to start a fight. I asked him to stop pushin' on me. I didn't want to fight. I hate fights. But he didn't stop, and before I knew anything, I was goin' home with a bloody nose.

"I cried all the way home. I couldn't help it. But soon as I got to my door, I stopped. I didn't want Mama to know nothin' had happened. I told her I ran into a door or somethin', I don't remember."

Jim Jim stopped talking all of a sudden.

"What's wrong, Jim Jim?" He looked down at the table.

"I never told nobody this before."

"Oh," I said. I understand secrets like that. "But it's half told already. And I promise not to tell anyone else. Cross my heart," I said.

Jim Jim nodded and went on.

"Well, when I got to school the next day, Tyrone had told everybody I was a punk. Then, pow!

Everybody started pickin' on me and I got pushed around and slapped around almost every day for a week.

"I went home cryin' most days 'cause I still wouldn't fight back. Then, one day I ran into Big Lil. She saw me cryin' and grabbed me and sat me down on the stoop and made me tell her what was the matter. I told her and she kinda hugged me, you know, and told me to dry my face. Then she said for me to listen. She told me how sometimes you have to fight, even if you don't want to, just to keep people from pickin' on you. She said I didn't have to fight everybody and I said I was glad of that. She said all I had to do was fight one person and pretend like I was mean to all the rest, and nobody would bother me anymore.

"Well, I knew who that one person was. Tyrone. Everybody in the first grade was scared of Tyrone. Everybody in the second grade too. Besides, Tyrone was the one who started everybody else pickin' on me.

"So when I went to school the next week, I went lookin' for Tyrone. He came over to me in the school yard and said he heard I was lookin' for him. I said, 'Yeah, do you still want to fight?' He started laughin' and I punched him in the stomach. That made him stop laughin', all right, and we ended up rollin' all over the ground.

"After that, if anybody even looked at me out the side of they eye, I looked mean. And you know, Big Lil was right. Nobody bothered me after that.

"The grown-ups don't like Big Lil much," said Jim Jim. "They think she's just a bad woman. But she's all right. I don't know, though—sometimes I get tired of pretendin'."

Jim Jim looked at me with a sort of sad smile, a little embarrassed. I didn't mean to make him feel bad like that, so I tried to change the subject. I pushed my plate of chop suey closer to him.

"I can't eat that stuff. You finish it, it's your favorite. And hurry up. The bell's gonna ring in a minute," I said.

Jim Jim smiled like he was saying thank you, and dug into the food.

School was out. The year
had gone pretty fast with all the moving and getting to know people from scratch. By summer I
knew almost everybody on the block, at least by
name. I knew most of the kids in school too, but I
wasn't hardly friends with none of them except
for Jim Jim.

The other kids were all right, but I was kinda

quiet and never had much to say to them. I guess I liked Jim Jim best 'cause he mostly stayed to himself like I did.

But me and Jim Jim still had a long way to go. There were all these tests you had to pass before you could really trust someone and call him friend. Like the first time he dared me to push him to see if I had any guts. And the time he told me that Mary Lee's sixteen-year-old sister was having a baby and that it was a secret, and it really wasn't a secret, 'cause he just wanted to find out if I'd tell. And the time I started a fight with big Butch and told him that Jim Jim was gonna beat his butt for messing with me and then waited to see if Jim Jim was gonna punk out. And the time I jumped in the river.

There was a park across the street that we played in all the time. It had swings and seesaws and all that other kiddy stuff, but Jim Jim and I just went there to play ball and climb the rocks that led to the river.

A fence separated the rocks from the rest of the park and kept all the little kids near the sandbox and all, but the rest of us could jump the fence without half trying.

We had a stickball game going one day. Pee Wee was on second base, Jim Jim was on third, and it was my turn at bat. I swung right past the ball the first time and everybody booed. But the second time that ball came at me I hit it clean over the fence. I was running my fool head off, saying, "Go on, Pee Wee, go on, Jim Jim. Make it home, I'm comin'!" Then I noticed that everything had sort of stopped. Everybody was looking at me kinda mean out the sides of their eyes.

"Hey, Pump!" screamed Sam. "What you have to hit the ball over the fence for? Now we can't find it."

"That's why I can't stand playin' with no girls," said Speed.

"Aw, Speed," said Pee Wee. "Why don't you stop? Bein' a girl ain't have nothin' to do with it. You hit the ball over the fence last week, remember?"

Speed shut his mouth. We all jumped the fence and looked for the ball. But we couldn't find it anywhere in those craggy rocks. We got tired of looking and gave up. There were plenty more balls, and besides, it was summer. We could always finish the game the next day. Everybody went back to the playground part of the park but me and Jim Jim. We decided to climb down to the bottom rocks by the river where it was cool.

I'd been wanting to go for a swim all day, but Jim Jim was afraid of the water so I hadn't said anything about it. But my clothes were sticking all to me, so I changed my mind. I took off my shoes and stuck my toes in first to see if it was good and cold. It was.

"What you doin'?" asked Jim Jim, plopping down on a rock.

"What's it look like?" I said.

Jim Jim picked up a piece of stick and started drawing something in the dirt. He looked up serious.

"You know you ain't supposed to swim here."

"Who said?"

"Your mama."

"Mama ain't here." I said.

"The sign, then." He pointed to a green-and-white painted wood sign sticking out of the dirt.

"Last week you said I couldn't read."

Jim Jim rolled his eyes and went back to his drawing.

"Anyway," I teased, "you just said that 'cause

you scared to get in yourself."

Jim Jim's face puffed up red, but he just kept on drawing. I jumped in.

"Wheeeee!" I screamed. I stuck my head under the water and stayed there till I couldn't hold my breath any longer. I came up splashing and slapping the water with the stiff palm of my hand. Jim Jim wasn't in the water, but he sure was good and wet by the time I finished.

"Come on in." I laughed. "The water's fine." Jim Jim just shook his head no. He was busy digging up worms to throw at me 'cause he knew how icky I thought they were. That's when the idea hit me.

The water was only up to my waist. I walked out a little farther and started splashing and coughing at the same time.

"Help! Help!" I screamed. Jim Jim looked up.

"Help! Help!" I screamed again.

Jim Jim shot up and took two steps to the edge of the river and stopped. He looked down at the water and I could see the fear in his eyes. Then he looked at me as if he was discovering me for the first time. I coughed and spluttered and went under. When I came up the next time, Jim Jim was waist-deep in the river, coming to me fast. I was still flapping around, but I had stopped coughing. Jim Jim was up to his shoulders. I stood up straight in the water and smiled. Jim Jim stopped dead. The water was up to his neck. He looked down at the river that had swallowed up more than half his body. He opened his mouth, but nothing came out. I couldn't hold it back. I laughed for all the world to hear.

"Cat got your tongue, Jim Jim?" I said.

"You ain't drownin'," he said. "You ain't drownin', Pump." Jim Jim said it over and over again to make himself believe it, and there I was laughing till the fear came back to his eyes.

"Aw, Jim Jim," I said. "Don't be afraid. It's only water. Come on." I took a step forward toward him. He took a step back.

"Don't be like that, Jim Jim," I called. "I bet you're a real good swimmer, too," I said. He took another step back and went under. I saw him waving and kicking and thought he was playing for a minute. Then I walked to the spot where he was standing and got pulled under too. There's a point in the river where the current switches. Jim Jim had walked right into it and I had followed. Now the river was pulling every which way and filling our lungs to bursting and taking us deeper. Jim Jim was flapping and kicking and spitting out water. He wasn't swimming. Jim Jim really couldn't swim. He was gonna save me from drowning and he couldn't even swim. And neither could I.

I felt around in the water for Jim Jim's hand. I found it and held on to it like life. It was life. Jim Jim's hand.

"Stand up! Stand up!" I yelled. "Pull, Jim Jim!" Jim Jim pulled. He stood up and was pulled back down. He got on his feet once more and dug his toes into the sandy earth and fought the current. He held my hand and he pulled. Again he was dragged down. His head bobbed up, his eyes shooting from left to right along the riverbank. He turned to look at me. The fear had gone from his eyes.

"It's O.K., Pump," he said. "It's O.K." Then he disappeared underneath the water. He'd felt something. I didn't know what, but I kept holding on. Jim Jim had been under the river for a long time. I started worrying. Was he all right? Nobody could hold their breath that long.

I felt a tug on my hand. Jim Jim was moving and he was pulling me. He still hadn't come up for air, but he was moving forward. One step at a time. And he was pulling me with him. His head finally came up out of the water. The water was only waist deep now, but only Jim Jim's head was above the water. He was leaning to one side and seemed to be holding on to something. When we were almost back on dry land, I could see what he'd been holding on to. A tree root. Thank God for tree roots, I thought. My eyes followed the root from where we stood in the water to the tree itself. The tree was just near the edge of the riverbank. That's what Jim Jim had felt when he turned to me and said, "It's O.K., Pump. It's O.K."

Jim Jim plopped down on the ground, pulling me down with him. He still held my hand. I stared down at it. Warm. Brown. Strong. Jim Jim's hand. It was life.

We sat quiet, catching our breath, easing out the fear and the shock in long deep sighs. Jim Jim broke the silence.

"Hey, Pump," he said. "I thought you could swim."

I laughed inside, and that deep-down laugh

pushed its way to my mouth and out and spilled all over that riverbank.

That's when Jim Jim and I became friends. That's when I told him that I wrote poetry and he told me that he liked to draw. And that's when I finally told Jim Jim about Daddy and about how it was with Mama and me.

The testing was over. The trust was true and setting in and we settled down to being as close as two sides of one coin. Yeah.

Me and Jim Jim had a lot of fun that summer. It turned out Big Lil knew how to swim so she taught us. Then we musta gone swimming a zillion times a week. It was nice. Even Jim Jim thought so, once he got past being scared.

We went to a picnic on July 4th with the church around the corner and we saw three movies. But before we knew anything, summer was over and school had started up again.

One day, Miss Morris was going over contractions. It was the third time that week we were going over the same lesson 'cause some kids just couldn't get it. English was my best subject, so I got it the first time, back in the fourth grade. By the third day, I was so sick of contractions I didn't even bother turning to that page in my workbook. Instead, I stood my workbook up on my desk so Miss Morris could see the cover, then I opened up my notebook behind it. While everybody else was doing the lesson, I was writing a poem. I heard Miss Morris start off the lesson with the words "could not."

"Joyce," called Miss Morris. "What is a contraction? Tell the class."

"A contraction is when you take two words and make one word out of it."

"Out of *them*," said Miss Morris. "O.K. Now how would you contract the words 'could not'?"

"C-O-U-L-D-N-apostrophe-T."

"And what does that spell?"

"Couldn't."

"Correct," said Miss Morris. "Now write it on the board."

While Joyce was writing, the teacher called on another student to contract the words "would not." By the time she got to the fourth word, I was so into my poem that I didn't know what was going on in class. I was thinking hard on the last line when I felt a tap on my shoulder. I jumped clean outa my seat. It was Miss Morris. She held out her hand for my notebook of poetry. She stuck the book under her arm.

"Now," she said. "Since we all know how much attention you've been paying in class, you may contract those last words."

I squirmed in my seat. Then I cleared my throat.

"Well?" snapped Miss Morris. "Don't keep us waiting all day!"

I cleared my throat again. "I don't know what the last words were, Miss Morris," I mumbled.

I was wishing I was invisible and feeling hot all over when Betty Warren shot up out of her seat. "I know the answer, Miss Morris," she said.

"Yes, Betty?"

"Can't. C-A-N-apostrophe-T. Can't." Betty's smile nearly stretched to the back of her head. I gave her a dirty look when she sat down.

Miss Morris started back toward the front of the class. Then, for no reason I could tell, she turned real quick and called on Jim Jim sitting in the chair next to me.

"Jim Jim!"

Jim Jim liked to went through the ceiling, he jumped up so fast. He moved so fast he accidentally knocked his notebook on the floor. He went to reach for it, but Miss Morris stopped him short.

"Leave it!" said Miss Morris. While Jim Jim and everybody else watched her, she walked to where the book had fallen and picked it up. She looked down at his drawing. Then she looked up at Jim Jim. He tried to smile a little, but she wasn't smiling back. She tore the page in half.

"Jim Jim, you and Pump," she said, looking at me, "can stay after school today. You will write one hundred times each, 'I will pay attention in class.' "

"But, Miss Morris," I grumbled, "I promise I won't do . . ."

"That's all! One hundred times. I won't discuss it anymore! Now, the next words are 'have not.' George, how would you contract those words?"

Me and Jim Jim sort of slumped in our seats for the rest of the class. Finally the bell rang to go home. Miss Morris sent us to the blackboard and made us start writing before she left. Betty hung around until everyone else had gone. Then she did a nasty little singsong on her way out of the class.

"Have f-unnn, you twooo." I sucked my teeth, but Jim Jim just ignored her.

Jim Jim was at the board in the front of the class and I was at the one on the side. We were both busy writing. Nobody said anything for a long time. I got bored just writing the same thing over and over again, so I started up talking.

"Hey, Jim Jim."

"What you want?"

"I want to talk."

"I don't want to talk to you."

"Why not?"

" 'Cause I'm mad at you. That's why."

"Mad at me? What'd I do?"

"What'd you do? If it hadn't been for you, I'da never got in trouble. And if I hadn't got in trouble, I wouldn't be here now, writin' this stupid sentence!"

"Just how you figure that?" I asked. "I didn't tell Miss Morris you were drawin'."

"Naw. But if you hadn't got caught writin' that poem, she wouldn't a thought about callin' on me."

"Well, didn't nobody tell you to knock that book on the floor so everybody could see what you were doin'," I said.

"Yeah, but I was nervous."

"Well, if you were nervous, then don't go

blamin' me. You and your nerves got you in trouble. *I* didn't."

I was hot. I rolled my eyes at Jim Jim and turned back to the blackboard. After a few minutes, he tried talking to me.

"Pump."

I didn't answer.

"Pump, I'm sorry."

I still didn't say anything.

"Pump, I said I'm sorry. What more you want?"

I softened up a little and turned away from the board. I still wasn't smiling, but Jim Jim could tell I wasn't so mad anymore.

"What was that you were drawin'?" I asked.

"A picture of Miss Morris. She so ugly, I guess that's why she tore it up." Me and Jim Jim laughed at that.

"Yeah," I said. "Did you see what she did with my poetry book?"

"She put it in her desk. But I don't know if she locked it," said Jim Jim.

I tiptoed to the door and stuck my neck out to make sure no one was around. Then I tiptoed over to the teacher's desk and slid open a side drawer. There was Jim Jim's picture torn in half and underneath was my poetry notebook.

"Let me see what you wrote," said Jim Jim. I thought about it for a minute. I hadn't shown Jim Jim any of my poetry before. I didn't hand it to him right away. I thought maybe he would laugh. And then I thought, Naw, Jim Jim wouldn't laugh. And then I thought, Well, if he does, I'll never speak to him again. Then I handed Jim Jim the book.

He scrunched up his forehead like he did whenever he was doing something serious, and read.

Find it hard believing God is dead.
If He was, this would be the next life.
Somehow I can't imagine Him being
    a practical joker.

I stood rubbing my hands together while he read. When he finished I thought he was gonna laugh for sure, the smile spread so fast across his face. But he didn't. He just smiled and looked at me like he was glad I was his friend. Then I looked real close at his drawing and I had to look at him the same way.

"Wow!" I said. "You can really draw, Jim Jim."

"Yeah, and you can really write too, Pump."

"Yeah. And I can really tell Miss Morris that you didn't finish your assignment." Me and Jim Jim just about jumped out of our skin. It was Mrs. Lee, our last year's teacher from down the hall. She hadn't made a sound coming into the class.

Me and Jim Jim put the notebook and drawing down on the desk and ran back to the blackboards. Mrs. Lee stood watching until we had written the sentence six more times. Then she disappeared.

We didn't do too much talking after that. We just finished as quick as we could and went home.

Miss Morris didn't know it, but her punishment did just as much good as it did bad. In fact it was mostly good, 'cause me and Jim Jim got to share the things we love the best. And that counts for a whole lot.

A month had gone by since me and Jim Jim had got in trouble with Miss Morris. I was still writing poetry and Jim Jim was still drawing, but we were much more careful about getting caught.

School wasn't so bad by then, 'cause I knew everybody. Still, I was glad it was Saturday.

Mama went shopping and sent me to the Laundromat. Rita and Miz Warren, Betty's mother, were already there. So was Betty. She was standing next to her mother with her hands behind her back swinging like she was gonna recite something from assembly.

Rita was leaning against a washing machine with her arms folded. Miz Warren was standing in front of her, with her hands on her hips, doing most of the talking.

"You know the Davis boy, Tony? Well, they say he dropped out of school."

"Umph," said Rita.

"Not my Betty," said Miz Warren. "She brings home As and Bs, and she knows if she gets a C not to come home at all!"

Betty rolled her eyes at me and stuck her neck up in the air when Miz Warren said that. I knew I was gonna puke any minute.

"If Betty even thought about dropping out of school, she knows I'd spank her silly, don't you?" Miz Warren turned to her daughter.

Betty got all serious. "But, Mama," she said "you know I wouldn't do nothin' like that."

Miz Warren sucked her teeth. "*Anything!*" shouted Miz Warren. "The word is *anything*. Can't you talk better than that? What you think I'm sending you to school for!"

Just then Miz Warren noticed that everyone in the Laundromat was looking at her. She was too dark to turn red, but she did change color some.

"Now see what you did?" she yelled at Betty. "Now you got all these people lookin' at me and laughin'." Betty didn't say anything. She looked too scared. Her mother grabbed her hand and started dragging her through the door.

"See you later, Rita."

"Hello, Miz Warren," I said.

"Oh, hi, Pump," she said on her way out.

"Hello, Rita." Rita made all the kids call her by her first name. Mama said it was because she didn't want to feel old. She was divorced and had a grown son who was married. But she always kept real young boyfriends.

"Hello, Pump. You know Betty, don't you?" asked Rita.

I shook my head yes.

"I feel sorry for that poor child," said Rita. "She's an only child like you and she don't seem to have too many friends. You know her. Maybe you could tell me why."

"Well." I wasn't too keen on answering that question. "Betty's all right when she's by herself. It's when she's with grown-ups that nobody can stand her. She tries to act so prissy then, like she's better than everybody else. Just because her Mama run that old rickety beauty parlor down the street."

"Well," said Rita, "she got that honest and fair."

"What?"

"Never mind," said Rita. I shrugged my shoulders and walked past the row of machines till I came to an empty washer.

When all the clothes were in the machine, I went over to the window ledge and sat looking at the rain. Me and Jim Jim usually played handball on Saturdays after errands. But not with the rain. Mama said I'd have to stay in after I finished the laundry.

I looked at the clock. It would be a half hour till the clothes were ready to dry. So I decided to run up to Jim Jim's for a little while.

Jim Jim's brothers and sisters were in the kitchen having lunch. Jim Jim was in his room. He had told his mother he wasn't hungry so he could draw while everybody else was busy eating. He had locked the door so nobody could bother him. He opened it to let me in.

"Hey, Jim Jim," I said.

"Hey, Pump," he answered.

"What you doin'?"

"Drawin'."

"I can *see* that," I said.

"Then what you ask for?" Jim Jim grumbled.

I took off my raincoat and sat on the floor next to him. He was drawing a picture of his baby brother. Jim Jim liked to draw people. It was almost finished.

"What you gonna do when you finish?" I asked.

"Don't know." Jim Jim put the last touches on his picture. "What you doin' out in the rain, anyway?"

"I'm doin' the laundry. I just came over to see what you were doin'," I said.

"Nothin', now." Jim Jim took his drawing to the dresser and set it down.

"I can see that," I said for the second time.

"Let me think," said Jim Jim, all serious. He plopped down on the bottom bunk bed.

"We can't play ball 'cause it's rainin'."

"Nope." I had an idea. "Let's watch TV."

"Uh-uh," Jim Jim said, making an ugly face.

"Why not?"

" 'Cause I don't feel like fightin' with everybody 'cause everybody wants to see somethin' different."

"Oh. I should have thought of that," I said.

Jim Jim was quiet for a long time. Then he said that he didn't have no ideas and I couldn't think of nothing either. So I got up and put my raincoat back on.

"Well, I guess I'll go back to the Laundromat and read a book while I'm waitin'," I said. He nodded. Then, when I was almost to the door, Jim Jim said it.

"Pump! I just had an idea! Why don't we make a book?"

"Huh?" I thought Jim Jim had just about gone crazy.

I took off my raincoat and forgot all about the laundry. Jim Jim rushed around the room taking out colored pencils and drawing pads and a pad for me to write on.

The kids were finished eating, but Jim Jim still had the door locked so they couldn't get in. We could hear them playing in the next room.

When Jim Jim had everything all set out, he sat down.

"O.K."

"O.K. what?" I said.

"Let's start."

"Well, what's this book gonna be about?" I asked.

"How am I supposed to know? *You* the writer!"

"Thanks!" I said. Just like Jim Jim, I thought. Take you right to the middle of something and leave you there.

What could I write a book about? The same thing you write poetry about, I answered myself. People I know and places I been.

I sat quiet for a long time not saying anything and started getting a little excited. Since Daddy died, Jim Jim was the only one I could show my writing to. He always took me serious. Just like Daddy. That wiped away some of the hurt of missing Daddy and made his being gone a little easier to get used to. I started to write.

"Well?" Jim Jim wanted to know. "Well, what you writin'?"

I told Jim Jim to shush and kept on writing.

When I finished, I turned back to the first page and handed Jim Jim the pad. He read out loud:

Pump and Jim Jim were walking down the street one day after school when a strange-looking lady passed right by them and said, "Hello."

"Do you know who that was?" asked Jim Jim.

"No," said Pump. "I thought you knew."

They decided to find out who the strange lady was, so they ran down the street after her. When they caught up with her, they said, "Who are you?" She turned around so they could see her face.

"Who do I look like?" she asked.

Pump and Jim Jim looked at her. Then they looked at each other. They both said the same thing at the same time. "You look like Miz Warren."

"Then I am Miz Warren," said the lady. And she started to walk away.

"Wait a minute," said Jim Jim. "You're too short to be Miz Warren."

"I just shrunk, young man. I just shrunk," said the lady. And she turned to walk away again.

"But wait a minute," said Pump. "You're too skinny to be Miz Warren."

"I just lost weight, young lady. I just lost weight," said the lady. And she turned to walk away once more.

"Wait a minute!" Pump and Jim Jim said together. "Your voice is too high and squeaky. You *can't* be Miz Warren."

"Of course I can," said the lady. "But if you don't believe me, I'll take off my mask." Then she reached up to her face and snatched off the mask. Pump and Jim Jim couldn't believe their eyes. Underneath the mask she still looked like Miz Warren, but somehow they knew she wasn't. Then they got an idea.

"So you say you're Miz Warren, huh?" asked Jim Jim.

"So I am. So I am."

"And you're sure that's who you are?" asked Pump.

"Yes, I am. I'm sure."

"Well, then," said Jim Jim, "I guess that means you can't come play with us."

"Yeah," said Pump. "I guess that means you can't be our friend."

Then, all of a sudden, just like that, the lady who looked like Miz Warren turned out to be Betty.

"I want to play! I want to play!" she said. "I want to be your friend!"

Pump and Jim Jim made their faces look serious. First they didn't say anything. Then finally they said, "O.K. You can play with us and be our friend. But first you have to promise something."

"Anything!" said Betty. "Anything!"

"You have to promise never to make believe you're like your mother ever again."

"I promise," said Betty.

So they all went down the street to the school yard and played a game of handball.

I could tell from him smiling every now and then that Jim Jim liked the story. When he finished, he looked up and grinned at me.

"Gee, Pump. Just think! When I do the drawings and we put the whole book together, then I'll really have somethin' to take to school and show old dumb Miss Morris."

That made me think of Mama, 'cause now I had something special to show her, too. I was hoping that it would really make a difference. That maybe she would look at the book and say, "Pump, I like your story. You keep writing, hear?" But I didn't believe she would say that for real. I was just wishing.

"Oh!" I jumped up. I remembered the laundry. "I gotta go, Jim Jim." I grabbed my raincoat.

"Why you rushin'?"

"I forgot the laundry."

"Oh."

"See you later." I unlocked the door and left before he could say good-bye.

It had stopped raining by Sunday, so I went over to Jim Jim's. When I got there, he was working on the last drawing of the book.

I didn't talk, 'cause I didn't want to mess him up. I looked at the drawings he had already finished.

"Are you really gonna show it to Miss Morris?"

I asked Jim Jim after a while. He stopped drawing and thought about it.

Jim Jim doesn't pay much attention in class and he plays hookey a lot. It's not 'cause he's bad. He just likes to draw. It's just that he draws in school and Miss Morris calls him stupid or else he gets in trouble like that time we both had to stay after school writing on the blackboard. What did Miss Morris know anyway?

"No," said Jim Jim after a while. "She'd probably only half look at it, then say, 'Why don't you pay attention in class 'stead of drawing pictures for some silly ol' book?' I could just hear her. No, I ain't gonna show her no book. You?"

I knew Jim Jim meant was I gonna tell my Mama. I said No, and Jim Jim went back to his drawing.

When he finished, we borrowed a stapler from next door and put the book together.

Jim Jim had rewritten the story in big block letters and did all the pictures in bright colors. He had drawn the apartment houses and the projects and the people and even remembered to put in the fire hydrants on the street.

Jim Jim looked kinda sad. I could see he was

thinking what I was thinking.

"Sure is a beautiful book, Jim Jim," I said.

"Sure is."

"Too bad we can't show it to nobody," I said for both of us.

"Yeah," said Jim Jim. "Too bad." We both got quiet.

"Well," I said after a while. "It's O.K. We know we did it." I smiled so Jim Jim would know I meant it and maybe smile back.

"Yeah, that's right," said Jim Jim. "We did it."

And you know, he did smile back.

Jim Jim kept the book
over at his house 'cause I didn't want Mama to
see it. We did two more books together right after
that. One was a comic book and the other was for
Jim Jim's little sister Ruth, for her birthday. She
had turned six and was just learning how to read.

We would have done more, only we didn't have

a place to do it all the time. Usually Jim Jim had to go home after school to watch his little brothers and sisters so we couldn't go to my house. That was too bad, 'cause Mama didn't get home from work till six. Sometimes we played hookey and went to the park. That worked O.K. while it was still warm, but we were gonna have to find somewhere else when it got cold.

"Pump. Hey, Pump."

I jumped down from my chair and ran to the kitchen window. It was Jim Jim, of course. He called for me every morning. We went to school together. When we went.

"Hey, Pump, ya ready?" Jim Jim yelled up from the street.

My mouth was full of soggy cornflakes, so I just shook my head no.

"Well, hurry up," he said. "I got a surprise." And he disappeared into the building next door. I stood at the window for a minute.

"Pumpkin, are you eatin'?" Mama asked from the other room. I ran back to the table and shoved a spoonful of flakes in my mouth.

"Yes, Mama," I said. I didn't like to lie. I turned the bowl up to my mouth and drank in the rest of the cereal, jumped down from the table, and grabbed my books. " 'Bye, Ma," I called over my shoulder, still chewing my food on the way to the door.

"How many times have I told you . . ." I was halfway down the stairs before Mama could finish the sentence.

When I got outside, Big Lil was on the stoop, leaning against the railing. Chilly as it is on October mornings, Lil had on the same skinny halter blouse she wore on July Fourth. Her clothes were always too something—too short, too thin, or too little, like a halter top on a cold October morning. But I liked Big Lil.

"Mornin', Miss Lil."

"Hi, Pump. On your way to school, huh?"

I screwed my face up like a prune. "Yeah."

Big Lil held me by the shoulders and bent over until our faces almost touched. "You don't sound too happy 'bout goin' to school. But you keep right on. Nice girls go to school so they can be nurses and teachers, and like that. If you don't go to school, you might end up like . . ." Big Lil shut her mouth tight, not finishing the sentence, and looked at the ground.

"Like what, Miss Lil?" I asked, guessing that she meant like her.

"Never mind, Pump. You just finish school for me, O.K.?"

"Sure, Miss Lil," I said, half shrugging my shoulders like I had missed something and didn't know what. But it didn't make a difference to me how she made her living. She was always kind to people, especially children. And Daddy had always said that that was what counted.

"Hey, Pump." Jim Jim ran up to the stoop and plopped down on the first step.

"Yeah." I picked up my books. "What's the surprise?" Jim Jim put his fingers to his lips for me to shush.

"Mornin', Miss Lil." Jim Jim smiled. Miss Lil smiled back.

"Don't make yourself late for school, Pump."

"I won't, Miss Lil." We watched Big Lil disappear into a building across the street. When she was out of sight, Jim Jim took my books, put them on top of his, and tiptoed into my hallway. Soon he was back on the stoop sitting next to me. But the books were gone.

"What ya do with the books, Jim Jim?"

"Come on," he whispered. I didn't know what he was up to, but I sure intended to find out.

There weren't too many people in the street that early. Truth is, the only person out was Popcorn, who was at the corner singing up a breeze as usual. Mama said he made some records once, but they never gave him his money. He used to sing and whistle and laugh in the daytime. But sometimes he drank too much at night. Then he'd scream at anybody who talked to him and he'd sit on his stoop and cry.

When we got to the corner, Jim Jim and me joined Popcorn in a squealing chorus of "A Fork in the Road" by the Miracles. We all laughed at how flat we sounded. Popcorn waved good-bye to us and we walked on.

There was no sign of old Mr. Banks that morning. Old crazy Mr. Banks.

When we reached the next block, Jim Jim pointed to the left. The school was to the right. Jim Jim looked around to make sure we weren't being watched and broke into a run.

"Come on," said Jim Jim. But he still hadn't told me just where we were going, and just what we were going to do. I wasn't running after Jim

Jim and his surprise until it wasn't a surprise anymore. At least, that's what I told myself. I had turned from Jim Jim and was walking the other way toward school. But I was stopped before I got half a block away.

"Hey!" yelled Jim Jim. "Lemme down! Lemme go!" His feet were dangling a foot above the sidewalk. Old Mr. Banks held him in the air by his collar. Old crazy Mr. Banks.

Mama said he used to have a fine job teaching in a college. Now he was our super, but he still called himself professor. He stood on the corner most of the time, with his eyes looking wild, talking to himself about the old days. He didn't always live in the neighborhood. Popcorn told me that when Mr. Banks was young he lived in another neighborhood, in another house with his wife. Popcorn said it was a very old house and that one day Mrs. Banks fell through a weak floorboard, broke her neck, and died. Mr. Banks had always been after the landlord to fix those boards, so when he found out, he killed the man and they sent him to jail. He finally got out, but Popcorn said he'd been acting crazy ever since he lost his wife.

I didn't know if it was true. Maybe he was crazy, maybe not. Nobody wanted to find out, least of all me and Jim Jim. But like it or not, I was gonna have to say or do something to Mr. Banks, 'cause Jim Jim looked like he was gonna turn purple from hanging in the air so long.

I ran up behind Mr. Banks and jumped on his back.

"Lemme down!" yelled Jim Jim. Mr. Banks was so busy turning around trying to get me off his back that he set Jim Jim on the ground. As soon as he did I jumped down, and we took off at a run. But Mr. Banks had a reach as fast as it was long and had us both by the shoulders in no time.

"Where you kids goin'?" demanded Mr. Banks.

"Let us go!" yelled Jim Jim.

"Why don't you leave us alone?" I added. "We ain't botherin' nobody."

He let go of us gently. Jim Jim brushed his jacket off as though old Mr. Banks had left a spot on it from holding him up in the air. There wasn't any spot. Jim Jim was just trying to cover up how scared he was.

"Y'all go on to school now," ordered Mr. Banks. We turned in the direction of the school this time, and started walking. Once we were out of Mr. Banks's reach, Jim Jim turned around and started bad-mouthing him.

"Why, you old greasy bum. Who are you, tellin' us what to do? If you weren't so big, I'd . . ." My hand flew up to Jim Jim's mouth.

"Shut up!" I hissed. "You want to get us in bad trouble? Let's get out of here before somebody else sees us. O.K.?" Jim Jim shook his head yes. Old Mr. Banks was still watching us, so we crossed the street and went into the school building. We walked through the hall to the back of the school, ducked past our classroom, and ran down the back steps to the basement. We tiptoed through the room holding our breath. Finally we reached the exit. Jim Jim turned the knob slowly. The door creaked when it opened. Maybe we were very quiet and maybe the door was very loud. To us, it sounded loud enough to wake up the dead. We got outside and ran as though someone was after us. When we stopped we were a good four blocks away. We stood under a lamp post, panting.

I caught my breath first. "O.K., Jim Jim. Since playin' hookey was your big idea, what are we goin' to do now? We can't run all day, you know."

I wasn't too happy with Jim Jim at that moment. "Anyway," I said, "what's so surprisin' about playin' hookey? We've done that before."

"That's not the surprise, dummy. I got somethin' to show you. Somethin' I been savin' up."

Jim Jim had this secret smile on his face that made his mouth kind of crooked. I couldn't tell much of anything from that look of his. I decided to trust him for a little while anyway. But just for a little while.

He led me across the street to an abandoned building and started inside. I jerked my hand away from him. "You're *not* goin' in there?" I asked. Jim Jim had a holding-in smile when he was trying not to laugh at you. He looked at me with that smile then.

"What's the matter, Pump? You scared?" Jim Jim taunted. He knew I was scared. I looked at that rickety old building with windows all knocked out and boards lying all over the place where people could trip and I must have turned three different colors. But I didn't care if he did laugh. I wasn't going in there.

"You can go in there if you want to, Jim Jim," I said. "But I'm not." Jim Jim broke down and laughed, but he didn't give up. He knew how to get me to go inside.

"Aw, Pump. It's safe in there. Honest."

"Uh uh. Nope. Ain't goin'." I stuck to my guns.

"I tell ya, I been in there plenty of times. Nothin' ever happened to me. Did I ever lie to you?"

I almost choked when he said that.

"O.K. So I've exaggerated once or twice. But this time I'm tellin' the absolute truth."

"No, Jim Jim. I don't like the way this place looks."

Then Jim Jim took a deep breath and said the one thing that could get me inside of that abandoned building.

"I dare you."

Jim Jim knew that I never backed down from a dare.

There were cobwebs hanging from the doorway and more in the hall. The banister from the stair had been knocked down and we had to hug the wall to keep our balance when we climbed the steps. I didn't see much of the first floor, nor of the second. Jim Jim kept climbing up. But then, there wasn't much to see. The rooms were mostly empty, with a few pieces of dusty, broken furniture and scraps of paper on the floor. All the doors were either falling off the hinges or torn off altogether. It didn't look too safe to me. No matter what Jim Jim said.

Jim Jim stopped on the third floor and took me to a room in the back. This was the only room I'd seen that had a working door.

"Open it," said Jim Jim with that secret smile on his face again. I opened it.

"Surprise," said Jim Jim.

This room had a window. And with curtains. And a bed and a closet, and even a stove with a teapot on it. Nothing in this room had that leftover look that everything else in the building had. And not one cobweb.

"Jim Jim! How did you find this room? Who lives here? Has he ever seen you? Why didn't you tell me about it before? Does anybody else . . . ?"

"Wait a minute," begged Jim Jim. "One question at a time." Jim Jim loved to see me excited. "I don't know who lives here. I didn't tell you before because I was keepin' it a surprise. And of course I didn't tell anybody else. Wait a minute." Jim Jim knelt on the floor and felt around underneath the bed. When he stood up he was holding a shoebox with an artist's pad and a stack of colored pencils and crayons. There was a pencil sketch on top. He handed it to me.

"Oh, Jim Jim! So this is the surprise!" It was a drawing of me. It was a little rough and I could see he hadn't drawn all the parts in yet, the lines and dimples and all, but it was beautiful. Jim Jim watched me smiling and looked like he was gonna bust from being so proud.

"Want to go up front?" he asked, taking the box and replacing it under the bed.

"Yeah. Race you," I said. "Get ready, get set, go!"

We ran down the hall. I was in front. Jim Jim might have caught up, but I had a head start. I beat him to the door and was halfway through the front room when Jim Jim screamed.

"Pump! Watch out!" But it was too late. Part of the floorboard was missing and my right foot went straight through it. My fall made a loud smack against the wood and I groaned. Jim Jim rushed over to me. His eyes had gone all soft and looked a little wet.

"Gee, Pump, I'm sorry. Are you hurt? I forgot about that board. You O.K.? Gee, Pump, I'm awful sorry. Here, let me help."

Jim Jim put his hand underneath one of my arms. With the other I pressed against the floor to give myself a push while Jim Jim pulled. Nothing happened. We tried again. Still nothing happened. Jim Jim walked behind me and put both hands underneath my arms. He tugged and tugged. I bit down on my lips. I didn't want to cry. My leg was stuck between two sharp pieces of wood. Every time Jim Jim pulled the wood scratched my leg. Jim Jim pulled one more time. Nothing happened. I was stuck and that was all.

"Pump, what are we gonna do? I gotta get you out of there." I didn't say anything. Jim Jim was already worried sick and I didn't want to make him feel worse.

"It's O.K.," I kept saying. "We'll think of somethin'."

We sat quiet for a while and Jim Jim calmed down. We thought about getting help. But that was no good. We were playing hookey and we weren't even supposed to be there. I asked Jim Jim to get a piece of rope to pull me out with like I'd seen on TV. But he said it probably wouldn't work. And besides, we couldn't find any rope. We tried to come up with another idea. Then I heard a sound from downstairs.

"Jim Jim. Do you hear somethin'?" He listened for a while.

"No. I didn't hear nothin'." The sound got louder. "Wait," said Jim Jim. "I do hear somethin'." Jim Jim's eyes grew wide as paper plates. "Someone's comin' upstairs," he whispered. There was nothing to do but wait. I was stuck. Jim Jim tried pulling me again. But it was no use. I couldn't get out.

The steps grew louder and louder. Jim Jim held his breath. I squeezed my eyes shut tight. We waited. The footsteps reached the door.

"What the devil are you kids doin' in here?"

I knew that voice. Right then I wished to God I didn't. I opened my eyes slowly. Mama always said you could tell when you were scared 'cause your skin felt all tingly. My skin was feeling like that then. It was the professor. Old crazy Mr. Banks.

"Didn't I tell you kids I didn't want to see your faces no more today?"

His voice crackled and bounced off the wall. The echo made him seem twice as mean. Jim Jim swallowed hard enough for me to hear. He was trying to find his tongue. Mr. Banks walked toward us. He stretched out his arm. Before Jim Jim knew what had happened, Mr. Banks had him lifted up by the shoulders and kicking his feet in the air for the second time that day. Mr. Banks kept shaking him and yelling with that wild look in his eyes.

"You don't belong here. Nobody belongs here. You shouldn't have come. You shouldn't have come. I'll teach you . . . I'll . . ." he kept saying. That's when I started screaming.

I thought sure we were gonna die right then. I swore to God if He got us out of this I would never play hookey again.

All of a sudden Mr. Banks stopped yelling and put Jim Jim back down, nearly dropping him. Then he did something real strange. He knelt down in front of me. His eyes lost that wild look, and for a minute he almost looked like he would cry.

"Are you hurt?" he asked softly.

Jim Jim passed me a look that told me he was as shocked as I. Neither of us spoke.

"Let's get you out of there. Son, you stay right here and watch her," said Mr. Banks to Jim Jim. "I'll be right back." He left the room. Jim Jim's eyes looked like they were gonna pop right out of his head.

"Did you hear that? He called me son. Old crazy Mr. Banks called me son!"

I told Jim Jim to shush. Mr. Banks had returned with a crowbar. He made Jim Jim stand back so that he would have enough space to work. He pried two of the boards loose. Before you could say Pump and Jim Jim, Mr. Banks had me out of that hole. Then he picked me up like a baby and carried me to the back room. His room.

He fished some change from his pocket and sent Jim Jim to the store for Band-Aids. Then he put a fire under the teapot.

When Jim Jim returned I was lying in bed with a rag soaked in hot water wrapped around my sore leg. Jim Jim handed the old man the can of Band-Aids and sat on the edge of the bed uncertainly. In all this time I hadn't said a word. I had been too afraid. But it didn't make much difference anymore. The worst was over. The tingly feeling of fear went away and I found my voice.

"Mr. Banks, thank you for gettin' me out of the hole and fixin' my leg."

Mr. Banks stood looking out of the window. I

don't even think he heard me. He was mumbling to himself the way he always did on the street corner. But I had never listened to him before.

"What did you say, Mr. Banks?" I asked.

"Willi Mae . . . she died like that . . . right through the floor . . . I told 'em to fix them boards . . . I told 'em . . . didn't I, Willi Mae . . . ?"

"What's he talkin' about?" Jim Jim asked me.

"They wouldn't listen . . . I told 'em . . ."

I sat up slowly and threw my legs over the side of the bed. I eased to the floor quietly.

"I'll tell you later, Jim Jim," I said in a whisper. "But now it's time to go."

Jim Jim pulled his shoebox out from under the bed. Then we took off our shoes so we wouldn't make any noise and left the room and the house to Mr. Banks.

I never told Mama 'bout
Mr. Banks. I wanted to, but things still weren't so
good with us. We were as different as people could
be and that's all there was to it, I thought.

I was on my way out the door one Saturday.
Mama heard the door slam and come running out
behind me.

"Pump Jackson, where you think you're goin'?
Get in here, girl," yelled Mama.

I hurried up and got inside. She only called me by my whole name when she was in a bad mood. 'Specially if it was something I did that put her in it. And I'd come in late the night before.

"Pump Jackson!" she said. "You're not goin' anywhere this day. Comin' in all hours. Since you're so smart, you can just stay home today and clean the house." Mama pressed her lips tight and left the room.

I was still standing by the door near the living room. I sucked my teeth, looked at the coffee table and the side tables and the bookcase, and thought about all that dusting and polishing and sucked my teeth again. This room will wait till last, I decided, and went to my own room to start cleaning there.

I didn't do much but take things from one place and put them in another to make it neater. I made a big fuss about putting all my books in place on the dresser, and must've smoothed over the bed a hundred times to put off doing the dishes and mopping the floor in the kitchen. Mama read my mind and figured I was stalling and called to me that I better get in that kitchen 'cause them dishes sure weren't gonna wash themselves and neither was that floor. I did the kitchen and looked under the sink for the rags to dust the living room.

The living room. I dragged into it, hating every stick of wood, every tabletop that stared back at me dull and needing polish and elbow grease. But dusting the tables wasn't so much. It was cleaning the bookshelves that spread tiredness all through my arms just to think about it. I had to take all them books down before I could even start. Then I had to put them back the same way I found them. I could only do one shelf at a time because I would forget which books came from which shelf. So I wasn't too crazy about doing the bookcase.

While I was scrubbing one of the tabletops, Mama came to the door.

"I'm goin' to the supermarket," she said. "When I get back, you be here."

I said nothing.

"Hear?" she asked a little louder.

"Yes," I said, and she was gone.

I picked up the piece of old towel we used for dusting and ran it over each tabletop, careful not to leave a speck of dust, else Mama would make me do it all over again. Mama still hadn't got back when I started on the bookshelves, so I decided to rest myself and flip through one of the books.

There wasn't much for me to read besides some old fairy tales Mama used to read to me when I was real little and a couple of readers from the last school year. I ended up looking through Mama's high-school yearbook and laughing, like I always did when I came to the picture of Mama as a young girl.

The book was kind of heavy for me and when I started to put it back on the shelf, it fell out of my hands. I picked up the book and saw that some papers had dropped out. The papers weren't pages from the book. They were poems. The first one was called "Do Birds Come in Silver?"

Rode in a silver bird
wasn't real though
no more than the men who made it
wrapped myself up in myself
as we left the ground for a while
was glad I had my blackness to cuddle up next to
'cause I was scared
and I wondered if I might get a look at God
and even if I didn't
I figured He'd get a better look at me.   R.B.

There were more. Each one was signed "R.B." Those were my Mama's initials before she married Daddy.

"Girl! What you doin'?" Mama's voice made me jump. It cut sharp and sudden through the quiet room.

"You're supposed to be cleanin', not readin'." Mama moved from the doorway taking the groceries to the kitchen. I put the poems back in the yearbook, finished dusting the bookcase, and put the rags in the hamper. Then I joined Mama in the kitchen. There were some oranges on the table. I reached for one and got my hand smacked.

"Not now," said Mama. "Dinner first."

I was wondering how to ask Mama about those poems I found, but I couldn't think of a good way, so I just said, "Mama, who is R.B.?"

"Who?"

"R.B."

"What makes you ask? You see those initials somewhere?" she asked.

"Yes. I found some poems in your old yearbook and that's the way they were signed."

Mama stopped putting away groceries and turned to look at me.

"When did you see those papers?"

"Today. Mama, why you lookin' at me so funny?" She waited a long time before she answered.

"R.B. stands for Renee Brown." Mama turned back to putting away the food.

I knew that. "Mama," I said, "that was *your* name before you married Daddy."

"Yes," said Mama quietly. She put away the last can of milk and folded up the brown paper bag. Then she came to the table and sat across from me.

"I know what you want to ask," she said. "Just listen and I'll try to explain." I didn't blink. I didn't even breathe. I just sat very still.

"When I was your age, I used to write poems and short stories. Everybody said I was gonna be a great and famous writer someday. And I believed them. Then, when I got older, I sent my poems out to magazines and publishing houses. But nothin' ever happened. Came time to make it on my own, all I knew how to do was write and type. Never wanted to know anything else. So today, I work for an insurance company, typing."

So. But what does that have to do with me? I thought.

"Did you stop writin'?" I asked.

"Yes."

"Why?"

"Because it hurt to have my work turned down. Because I failed."

"But I won't fail Mama," I said. "And even if I do, I have to try."

Mama studied me across the table, her eyes wet and smiling at me with love.

"I guess you're right, chile. I guess you're right."

We were closer after that. When Daddy was alive, we'd shared him. Now he was gone, we had something else to share. We both loved to write.

I remembered Daddy saying that day we were playing handball, just before he died, "Your mother loves you, Pumpkin. Just as much as I do. Maybe more. . . ."

After that me and Mama got along O.K. She made a big deal about having a talk every day when she came home from work. We'd talk about what she did that day and what I did in school. Some of it was kinda silly, but some of it helped us to know each other more.

We talked about writing a lot. One day she asked me why I started writing. I told her that I couldn't talk to people out loud too good, but I could always say just what I wanted to on paper. The words and feelings never got jumbled up in a poem. It kept me from hurting people too, I said. Most times when I got mad at somebody, I'd write an angry poem instead of yelling at the person who made me mad. Mama said she liked to write poetry 'cause it was one of the beautiful things in life.

She showed me the poetry she had kept and I read her mine some nights. It got so me and Jim Jim could work right at my house on weekends and Mama would even turn down the TV.

Things weren't the same as when Daddy was around, but I didn't expect them to be anymore. What counted was that I loved Mama and she loved me.

Mama wasn't the only one who loved me. I hadn't really thought about it much, but there were all those people on my block who'd come to care about me too.

'Specially Big Lil. It had got so I was one of her favorite people, along with Jim Jim. Me and Jim Jim kinda thought she was something too. But seemed like we were by ourselves, 'cause the adults didn't have no use for Big Lil. No sir.

"Chile," Miz Warren said one day, "that Lil thinks she's Miss It. Shakin' her butt every time a man passes by."

"Well, Shirley, whatcha want?" asked Rita. "That's how she makes her livin'."

"Humph! You'd think she'd have some shame, that no-good hussy. She oughta . . ." Just then Popcorn passed.

"Why don't y'all quit talkin' about that chile?" Popcorn cut in. "You can't judge no book by the cover. And according to the Good Book, you ain't supposed to judge nohow."

"Humph," Miz Warren grunted a second time. Rita said nothing. Miz Warren looked down at her watch.

"Well, it's time for me to be gettin' on downtown now anyway. See you later, Rita. I'm not even speaking to you, Popcorn," she added, heading for the bus stop. Popcorn just laughed.

Jim Jim and I had been playing lodies in the street, listening while all this talk was going on. I didn't think too much of their conversation, and neither did Jim Jim.

"I wish people would stop bad-mouthin' Big Lil," I said.

"Yeah," said Jim Jim. "They oughta just mind their own business. That's what makes me sick about people around here. Seems like all they know how to do is talk about somebody. If you went to them for help, they'd probably look at you like you were crazy!"

"Gee, Jim Jim," I said, surprised to see him all huffed up. "I didn't know you could get that mad."

"Well," said Jim Jim, cooling down a little. "I do. I wonder sometimes if folks could stop pickin' at each other and help each other, that's all." Jim Jim looked at me like I might have the answer. I looked back at him and shrugged my shoulders.

We finished our game of lodies and Jim Jim put his marbles into his pocket. We raced each other to school. We got there just in time to be late, as usual, right after the bell went off.

"One fifth of twenty is?" Miss Morris looked around the room for someone to answer. Scabby old Betty Warren, who thought she was the school genius, raised her hand all proper and sat there grinning all over herself until the teacher called her.

"Yes, Betty?" Betty stood up like she was gonna give a speech or something.

"One fifth of twenty is four."

"Thank you," said Miss Morris. "You may sit down now."

Betty took her time sitting down, still grinning like she was God's gift to the world.

"One fifth of twenty is four," said Jim Jim in a squeaky voice, copying Betty. I had to bust out laughing, he always sounded so funny talking like Little Miss Betty Warren. Right in the middle of my laugh, the school fire alarm went off.

"Uhh," everybody in class groaned.

"All right," said Miss Morris, putting down her chalk. "Line up by the door in two rows."

We all moaned and sucked our teeth and sort of dragged ourselves to the door.

"Come on," said Miss Morris. "We've all been through this before. You know we have a fire drill every Tuesday at the same time, so just line up and we can get it over with."

Jim Jim and I walked to the back of the line and stood side by side.

"Betty," ordered the teacher.

"Yes, Miss Morris?"

"You stand on the back of the line behind Pump and Jim Jim and make sure everybody stays in two rows."

"Yes, Miss Morris."

Jim Jim looked like he was gonna puke, and I rolled my eyes. Betty already thought she was Miss It. With her on the back of the line, all hot to report somebody, we probably couldn't sneeze without getting in trouble. But I guess it wasn't Betty's fault. She was just acting like her mother, Miz Warren.

All the kids were in line behind their teachers in the hall, waiting for their turn to march outside till the fire drill was over. It looked like we were gonna be standing there forever. Finally the line started to move. We were halfway down the stairs when the line stopped again. We stood there for a few minutes and I looked behind me. There was old smug-faced Betty Warren, but that was all. We were the last class going out. I let out a tired breath and turned back around. Jim Jim leaned over and whispered in my ear.

"We're gonna be here all day. Why don't we go to the music room and play lodies till the fire drill is over?"

I shrugged my shoulders to say O.K. We turned to go back up the stairs. Before Betty could open her mouth to ask where we were going, Jim Jim put his finger to his mouth for her to shush and shook his fist near her face so she would be too scared to say anything after we had gone. She looked mad, but she didn't dare say a word, so we tiptoed up the stairs and headed for the music room, running.

Jim Jim felt around for the light switch. There were no windows in the music room, so it was very dark. He turned on the lights and moved back the chairs to make a space on the floor to play. Just then we heard a noise in the hall. We went to the door to look. It was little Miss Betty Warren, come to spy on us.

We took a vote and decided Betty could stay, so we all played lodies for a while. I had beat Jim Jim, so I told him it was his turn to play my game. I took some chalk from the blackboard and made a hopscotch box in the front of the room. Jim Jim's mouth turned down and he backed up to the door.

"Jim Jim, where you goin'?" I asked. "I thought you wanted to play." He stuck his lip out and rolled his eyes.

"I ain't playin' no hopscotch. That's a girls' game." Betty giggled. I looked at her hard. She stopped.

"Don't be silly," I said, sucking my teeth. "Ain't nobody here to watch but us. And who said it was a girls' game anyway? Marbles is supposed to be a boys' game, but I just finished playin' it, didn't I?" Jim Jim stuck his hands in his pockets and hung his head down.

"O.K.," he mumbled to the floor. "I'll play. *This* time." We started playing and Jim Jim did look funny, but it was just that I hardly ever saw boys playing hopscotch. I kept fighting down a laugh 'cause I knew if I let it out Betty would start laughing too, and Jim Jim would just die.

We forgot all about the fire drill after a while, and we never knew what was going on outside since there weren't any windows. We heard something that sounded like a siren. We decided it was probably a police car and went back to our game.

Betty won two games of hopscotch and I won three. We'd let Jim Jim win a game, since he was new at it, so he wouldn't feel bad. But we were all getting tired of hopscotch by then, and getting hungry too. Nobody had a watch, but we knew that we should have heard that second bell a long time before then. We decided not to wait anymore. We'd go to the corner grocery store and get some donuts, then go back to class.

I took the blackboard eraser and wiped away the hopscotch box from the floor. Betty and Jim Jim put the chairs back, and I went to open the door. Just then, the lights went out.

"Hey, Pump, I gotta find my marbles," said Jim Jim. "Turn the light back on for a minute."

"I didn't turn it *off*," I said, disturbed. "Let's get out of here." I put my hand on the doorknob and pulled. The door was stuck.

Jim Jim tried the door. He thought maybe I was just too weak to open it. But nothing happened. That door was good and stuck and somebody was gonna have to break it in. The room was pitch black. There was no other way to get out. We all sat down to think.

"You know," Jim Jim said with hope, "we really don't have anything to worry about. It must be close to time for music class. Somebody will be comin' soon."

"Hey, yeah! That's right!" I said, all happy. "I forgot about that. You know . . ."

I felt Betty pulling on my arm and stopped talking. I thought she was gonna tear it right out of the socket.

"Over there," she yelled in a squeaky voice. She pointed my arm to the bottom of the door. I didn't see anything, but I smelled something funny. I bent down on my knees and sniffed. It was smoke.

Soon we could hardly breath in that room anymore. Jim Jim and I were choking and Betty had already blacked out. We screamed our fool heads off, but nobody was there to hear. We just knew we were gonna die. But we decided to keep screaming anyway, as long as we had some breath left. We counted to three and screamed together. That's when we heard Big Lil.

"Pump! Jim Jim! Y'all in there?" she yelled.

Jim Jim and I banged on the door, shouting, "We're here! We're here! The door is stuck!"

She shouted for us to move away from the door. We screamed back that we had and to please hurry. Suddenly we heard something crash through the door. Lil was breaking the door with an axe.

A few minutes later Big Lil led us outside, carrying Betty Warren in her arms. Everybody crowded around us all at once. Miz Warren was crying, bent over Betty. Mama was there too, crying, but she kept wiping the tears away and giving orders for everyone to make way for the ambulance people, and sending someone in the ambulance with Miz Warren to help her calm down and tell her that Betty was gonna be all right. Jim Jim's mother forgot all about him being man of the house and hugged him close with tears running down her face.

Once Mama saw Miz Warren and Betty off in the ambulance, she turned to Big Lil and asked how she happened to be at the school just after the fire started.

Turned out Big Lil's middle son, Mikey, had been acting up in school bringing his bean shooter to class, and throwing erasers and making all kinds of noise. Big Lil had talked to him about it and Mikey swore he'd stop doing those things. But this had happened before, so Big Lil decided to make a surprise visit to his class to see for herself if he was really keeping his word. 'Stead of surprising Mikey, though, she got the surprise.

When she got to the school she saw the fire

trucks and kids outside all lined up. Then she saw a lady running from one line to the next like she was looking for somebody. Lil asked the lady what was the matter. The lady turned out to be Miss Morris and she said three kids were missing. Lil still didn't know that me, Jim Jim, and Betty were the three kids. She thought maybe Mikey was one of them. So, she said, she closed her eyes and asked Miss Morris what the kids' names were. It wasn't Mikey, but it was almost as bad, 'cause Big Lil loved us near as much as she loved her own children. She decided right then that she was going in that school after us, no matter what any old fire chief said. And when no one was looking, she slipped in through a side door.

When Lil finished talking, Mama turned back to me. Lil disappeared during the rest of the commotion and we didn't see her again until we'd all gotten back from the hospital. That night everybody gathered at Miz Warren's house and made a fuss over me and Jim Jim and especially Betty. They brought food and beer and everyone was talking all at the same time.

Big Lil was sitting in a corner quietly, smiling to

herself. Miz Warren was in the kitchen taking cold beer from the refrigerator. Popcorn walked up behind her and tapped her on the shoulder. When she turned, he whispered something in her ear and she nodded.

She opened one of the beers and walked over to the corner where Lil was sitting. She stood over her silently, and the two women looked at each other for a long time without speaking. Then Miz Warren stretched out her arm to hand Lil the cold beer.

"What can I say?" whispered Miz Warren. Lil took the beer from her and sipped.

"Thank you," Lil answered. "And thank God. That's all anyone can say." Miz Warren fell to the floor and threw her arms around Lil's neck, crying and smiling. Jim Jim and I looked at each other and around the room at all the people who made up our world. From the soft look in Jim Jim's eyes, I knew that he was thinking the same thing I was.

These people weren't really so bad, when the hard times came. They were all good, feeling people. Popcorn, Rita, old crazy Mr. Banks, Miz

Warren and Big Lil, Jim Jim's mama, and my mama. . . . And besides, they were our folks. Jim Jim's people. Pump's people. And that made them all right.